Bad Ideas: They Came . . . and Fell on Their Faces

Call them "mental lapses"—
* I think my mother should come live with us. . . .
* Let's use *real* candles on the Christmas tree this year. . . .
* Hey, I've got it! We'll *vacuum* the cat. . . .

Foolhardy flops—
* New Coke
* *Ishtar*
* The Edsel

Bonehead blunders—
* "Smell-O-Vision" movies
* Polyester leisure suits
* Prefrontal lobotomies

Filled with hundreds of outrageous oversights, idiotic innovations, and preposterous proposals, this uproarious assemblage of ill-advised notions proves once more that to err this big can only be human.

It Seemed Like a Good Idea at the Time

LEIGH W. RUTLEDGE lives in Pueblo, Colorado, where he moved into a Victorian "handyman's special" that seemed like a good idea at the time. He is also the author of *Excuses, Excuses*; *The Left-Hander's Guide to Life*; *A Cat's Little Instruction Book*; and *Cat Love Letters*.

It Seemed Like a
Good Idea at the Time

*A Book of Brilliant Ideas
We Wish We'd Never Had*

LEIGH W. RUTLEDGE

A PLUME BOOK

PLUME
Published by the Penguin Group
Penguin Books USA Inc., 375 Hudson Street, New York 10014, U.S.A.
Penguin Books Ltd, 27 Wrights Lane, London W8 5TZ, England
Penguin Books Australia Ltd, Ringwood, Victoria, Australia
Penguin Books Canada Ltd, 10 Alcorn Avenue, Toronto, Ontario, Canada M4V 3B2
Penguin Books (N.Z.) Ltd, 182–190 Wairau Road, Auckland 10, New Zealand
Penguin Books Ltd, Registered Offices: Harmondsworth, Middlesex, England

First published by Plume, an imprint of Dutton Signet, a division of Penguin Books USA Inc.

First Printing, June, 1994
1 3 5 7 9 10 8 6 4 2

℗ REGISTERED TRADEMARK—MARCA REGISTRADA

LIBRARY OF CONGRESS CATALOGING IN PUBLICATION DATA
Rutledge, Leigh W.
It seemed like a good idea at the time : a book of brilliant ideas
we wish we'd never had / Leigh W. Rutledge.
p. cm.
ISBN 0-452-27189-4   I. Title.
PN6162.R85 1994   818'.5402—dc20   93–47647   CIP

Printed in the United States of America

Introduction: When Bad Ideas Happen to Good People

In college, I knew a girl who was once seeing off a roommate at the airport. As they were going through the security checkpoint at the entrance to the boarding area, the girl suddenly joked in a loud voice to her friend, "Go on, Linda—aren't you going to tell them about the gun you have stuffed in your bra?"

At a New Year's Eve party in 1985, I found myself talking to a man who had just taken his life savings out of the bank and planned to invest it in a company that was going to mass-produce Judd Nelson dolls. I thought he must be drunk. "No, no, I mean it," he told me excitedly. "This guy's the next James Dean! Think of all those teenage girls who are gonna want their own Judd Nelson doll. I'm gonna make a killing. . . ." Looking back on it now, I can't believe I maintained a straight face.

Last year, the Internal Revenue Service announced it was going to market a special commemorative Christmas ornament, as part of its program to try and "humanize" the tax service, an agency that's probably the most feared and loathed bureaucratic arm in Washington. Each sparkling golden ornament was to be engraved with the words, "Many Happy Returns, 1913–1993—Eighty Years of Income Tax." Price to the public: $11 each. Just what everyone wants hanging on their Christmas tree, right? A reminder of 1040 forms, interest penalties, and April 15. . . .

And you thought *you* had bad ideas sometimes.

This book is a tribute to bad ideas and the people who have

them, to inspiration gone awry. Right now, as you read this sentence, there are otherwise perfectly sane men and women all over the world who—with the best of intentions—have just put one foot on a banana peel and don't know it.

"I've decided to go into business with my brother. . . ."

"Now that she's finally out of the hospital, I think I'm gonna tell my wife about that affair I had with her sister last year. . . ."

"Stop worrying—my dad used to take this shortcut all the time when we were kids. . . ."

"If you've got a knife, I can pry the rest of this broken light bulb out of the socket for you. . . ."

"Hold on, everyone! We're going to try and beat the train across the railroad tracks. . . ."

By the time you've finished reading this entire book, someone, somewhere on the planet, will have turned to their mate and uttered the words, "I think my mother should come to live with us. . . ."

If you could see these people, you'd wince. And howl. (It's one of the truisms of bad ideas that everyone knows they're bad except for the people who conceive them.) And if they could see you tomorrow, when you innocently suggest a bribe to the highway patrolman or when you stick your hand down the garbage disposal trying to unblock it, they'd wince—and howl—as well.

The two girls at the airport? They spent several hours being strip-searched and threatened with one ominous federal law after another.

The man who invested in Judd Nelson dolls? He lost his shirt.

For most of us, bad ideas are an occasional aberration, a case of temporary insanity rather than a way of life. Each of us can take some small comfort in that.

Generally Bad Ideas

I've decided to see what I look like as a blonde. . . .

I've decided to go into business with my brother. . . .

I've decided to quit my job and go back to college to get a degree in medieval Hungarian literature. . . .

Now that she's finally out of the hospital, I think
I'm gonna tell my wife about that affair
I had with her sister last year. . . .

Come on, Doris—he's eleven years old, for
Christ's sake. What harm would it do if he drove
the car for a couple of miles? . . .

If I can just get my foot up on this last little limb,
I think I can almost reach the kite. . . .

Sure, he drinks too much and does cocaine; but
I'm sure I can change all that
once we're married. . . .

I know they haven't spoken since she
tried to run him over with the car. I just thought we
might help smooth things over by
inviting them both to dinner on Sunday. . . .

I think my mother should come to live with us. . . .

Well, it's cheaper than Morocco, and besides
my travel agent says the civil war is
over in Beirut. . . .

We've decided to get a boa constrictor as our next pet.
The guy at the pet shop says they're great with kids. . . .

Oh, don't worry—the puppy'll be fine
locked in the bedroom for a few hours. . . .

Hey, I've got it! We'll *vacuum* the cat. . . .

Of course, Harry and I keep the gun loaded and handy in
the nightstand. Who knows when one of us might
need it all of a sudden. . . .

6 Bad Ideas During the Holidays

1. Look, everyone—Harold has decided to come down the chimney just like a *real* Santa Claus. . . .

2. Listen to me, it's a great idea—we can send the Christmas cards we received last year, using whiteout to erase the original signatures. . . .

3. Hey, I know—let's use *real* candles on the Christmas tree this year. . . .

4. Carl and I decided we wanted to do a really honest and up-front Christmas letter this year, so we included everything in it—the marriage counselor, the miscarriage, little Tommy's breakdown, my mother's suicide. . . .

5. Call 911—*they'll* know what temperature you should cook the turkey at. . . .

6. Look, everybody—Leonard's wrapped the dog in Christmas lights. Go ahead, Leonard—plug them in! Let's light Muffin up. . . .

Hell, yes—just pile on another
helping of beans. . . .

Hell, yes—just pile on those jalapeños. . . .

Surprise! I decided to try anchovies and
peanut butter in the omelet this morning. . . .

Quit making those stupid faces—gasoline works
just as well as charcoal starter fluid. . . .

It's settled then: Florian if it's a boy,
Persephone if it's a girl. . . .

I went off the pill three weeks ago; I just
haven't gotten around to telling him yet. . . .

I guess you're right: If two people love one
another, they don't need to use a condom. . . .

The guy at the mechanic's shop says it isn't just the
clutch, that the car needs a whole new engine.
I think I can trust him. . . .

I went ahead and sent in that $250 processing fee
to claim the new car
those real estate people in Texas said I won. . . .

I know he's only five years old, but we decided to
go ahead and get him the dissection kit for
his birthday anyway. . . .

Hell, there's only a couple of inches of snow
out there. I don't need to shovel the sidewalk. . . .

Hell, I just throw all my old canceled checks
away. I mean, have *you* ever known
anyone who needed their old checks? . . .

Hell, it's just another parking ticket. What
are they gonna do—come to the
house and put me in *handcuffs*? . . .

Trust me—the IRS is *never* going to
figure out that the swimming pool
isn't a business expense. . . .

I know—let's dry the dog in the *microwave*. . . .

5 Bad Ideas at a Party

1. Hey, look everybody! Johnnie's going to open the beer bottle with his teeth. . . .

2. To hell with it—go get the Black & Decker and we'll *saw* the frozen patties apart. . . .

3. Oh for God's sake, I quit drinking six months ago. What harm is one little martini going to do me now? . . .

4. Come on, Martin, she'll never know. Go get
   Alice's diary. We've all been dying to
know what she writes about in that thing. . . .

5. Come on, George, ol' buddy—stop shaking or the
apple will fall off your head. What're you worried
about, anyway? I've seen 'em do this
dozens of times in the movies. . . .

Oh, who has time to read all the fine print. . . .

I think I'll have just one more for the road. . . .

If you'll remember to wake up in the morning, we won't have to use the alarm clock. . . .

Well, the bottle said to take two for a headache, so
I thought six would get rid of my headache
three times as fast. . . .

What do you mean I shouldn't have given him the credit cards? Has it ever occurred to you that maybe he wound up in prison the first time because no one ever trusted him? . . .

It was getting so late, I just copied the entire term paper from some old book I found in the library.
The professor's never going to find out. . . .

I have to go to Vegas this weekend to try and win enough money to make the house payment. . . .

Faster, Edith, *faster*!! We can outrun the
tornado if we really try. . . .

We don't *need* a sitter—I tell you, the baby'll
sleep right through the entire movie. . . .

We've decided to go ahead and buy the
Victorian fixer-upper instead of
the condo. . . .

Let's have the *biggest* wedding anyone's ever had.
After all, you only get married once. . . .

Well, he's got a friend whose brother bought some, and
he made a million dollars overnight. I mean,
how hard can it be, buying and selling pork bellies? . . .

What do you mean I'm a fool to go golfing during a thunderstorm? This is the perfect time—no one else is out there. . . .

Laundry detergent will work just fine in the dishwasher. After all, it's all soap, isn't it? . . .

Oh, don't bother turning on the light. I can find my way downstairs in the dark. . . .

I couldn't find the barber clippers, but here's those pruning shears Mom uses to cut the roses. . . .

Oh, don't worry about locking the car. After all,
this isn't New York or Los Angeles. . . .

I know the last three women he's set me up with
haven't exactly worked out. But he swears
this one is a sure bet. . . .

Surprise! I cleaned out your desk while
you were on vacation. . . .

6 Bad Ideas While on Vacation

1. Oh, come on, Ralph—the deer here are used to being fed by tourists all the time. They'll love the rest of your Burrito Supreme. . . .

2. Just a little farther back, Madge. I want to get a picture of you right on the edge of the cliff. . . .

3. Stop worrying—my dad used to take this shortcut all the time when we were kids. I know this part of New Mexico like the back of my hand. . . .

4. Go on, Howard—offer the policeman forty bucks. I bet he'll just throw the ticket away. . . .

5. I told my daughter she could have as many friends over as she wants while we're out of town. I mean, I don't want to seem like one of those moms who never let their kids *do* anything. . . .

6. Well, they seemed like such nice people, and I figured if they want to ride in my trunk from Guadalajara, who am I to say no? . . .

I've decided to get my nose pierced. . . .

I've decided to drop out of school. . . .

I've decided to take up flying lessons to try and get over my fear of heights. . . .

Instead of exchanging the usual vows, Slash and
I have decided to have each other's names tattooed
on our rear ends. . . .

Merle decided to take all our money out of savings and invest it in old beer bottles. Do you have any *idea* how much collectibles have appreciated in the last ten years? . . .

Good lord, I haven't paid income taxes in seventeen years, and no one's ever caught *me*. . . .

Hold on, everyone—we're going to try and
beat the train across the railroad tracks! . . .

We'll just wait until we get there to find
a motel room. . . .

Try soaking your hand in Clorox—that'll
take all the grease off. . . .

Oh, I don't think we need anything in writing.
Your word is good enough for me. . . .

Hey, Mary—can you balance the TV on the edge of
the tub here, so I can watch
the news while I'm taking my bath? . . .

Funeral or no funeral, I think it's time all these weepy
people knew what a rotten son of a bitch
he really was. . . .

Now that Frank's lost his job, we've decided to grow a little pot in the basement to help make ends meet. . . .

I *know* Randy doesn't know anything about cutting hair. But it'll save me twenty bucks, and besides, he can't do a worse job than those people at the salon do. . . .

Just put sunglasses on and pretend that Wolfie's
leading you—that way we don't have
to leave him in the car while we eat. . . .

I think it'd be easier to let the new secretary handle
all the bank deposits from now on. . . .

Oh, look—what unusual mushrooms! Here,
take a bite. . . .

I'll have that hamburger extra rare, please. . . .

7 Bad Ideas Around the House

1. If you hold the other end of the lawn mower, we can just pick it up and trim the junipers this way. . . .

2. Don't bother about a regular hammer. I've got a sledgehammer in the car. . . .

3. I can get my ex-brother-in-law to rewire the entire house for next to nothing. . . .

4. Oh, for God's sake, Alice—it's just a little wasps' nest. Go get me a shovel and we'll move it ourselves. . . .

5. If you've got a knife, I can pry the rest
of this broken light bulb out of the socket for you. . . .

6. Would you stop whining and get me a
screwdriver?! I mean, why the hell should we pay
some bozo at the video store a hundred bucks
to fix the VCR?! . . .

7. Just one more turn of the wrench and we'll make
triply sure that it's nice and tight. . . .

You don't mind if my mother tags along
on our date tonight, do you? . . .

I just decided it was time *someone* told her what everyone's really saying behind her back. . . .

Aw hell, don't worry about it—you can
pay me back whenever you feel like it. . . .

Mommy, I've decided to become a politician when
I grow up. . . .

If I can just get my hand down the
garbage disposal here. . . .

More Generally Bad Ideas

Smoking in bed . . . Sending explosives through the mail . . . Forgery . . . Embezzlement . . . Calling in sick when you're not . . . Storing rat poison in an old orange juice bottle in the refrigerator . . . Wearing a cheap toupee . . . Buying the "floor model" . . . Answering junk mail . . . Treating all red lights as stop signs after midnight . . . Answering computer-telephone solicitations . . . Inviting door-to-door

missionaries inside your house . . . Being late with
loan payments . . . Waiting five years between visits to
the dentist . . . Driving on low tires . . . Pretending
you're drowning to catch a cute lifeguard's attention
. . . Telling the emergency room staff you don't have
any health insurance . . .

Putting people more powerful than you on hold . . .
Trying to mark cards at the blackjack table . . .
Exaggerating on your résumé . . . Spying on the
neighbors . . . Talking all the time about your
miserable childhood . . . Hitchhiking to Hollywood to
become a star . . . Postdating checks . . . Not backing
up your computer data . . . Jumping to conclusions . . .

Digging up trees in national forests . . . Letting the
cat box go uncleaned for more than a week . . . Taking
antibiotics when you don't need them . . . Trying too
hard to be clever at dinner . . . Buying an extended
warranty . . . Talking with your mouth full . . . Sending
hate mail to John Gotti, in prison—and *signing* it . . .

Famous Bad Ideas

The Edsel

The Battle of Little Big Horn

Michael Jackson's plastic surgery

The Titanic

The Ford Pinto

Michael Dukakis for president

Anne Boleyn deciding to marry Henry VIII

Prince Charles confessing his erotic fantasies over
a cellular telephone

Going back for the rental deposit after trying to
blow up the World Trade Center

IT SEEMED LIKE A GOOD IDEA AT THE TIME #1

"We'll have a speaker system outside the camp, near the river. After a tour gets inside the camp, we'll broadcast a firefight, mortars exploding, bullets flying, Vietnamese screaming."

> —U.S. businessman Giles Pace, discussing an idea for a new multimillion-dollar amusement park, "New Vietnam," in Florida, in 1975

IT SEEMED LIKE A GOOD IDEA AT THE TIME #2

"I consider all possibility of danger in the new zeppelin eliminated."

> —Navy Lt. Comdr. Scott Peck, urging
> the U.S. to build zeppelins just like the
> recently completed, German-made
> *Hindenburg*, 1936

IT SEEMED LIKE A GOOD IDEA AT THE TIME #3

"These people would just abuse them."

> —A South African official, trying to justify
> why recently completed high-rise apartment
> complexes for blacks were built with no
> electrical outlets in them, 1972

Heaven's Gate

Howard the Duck

Prefrontal lobotomies

Zsa Zsa Gabor's first seven marriages

Klara Hitler wanting children

Milli Vanilli

Silicone breast implants

Platform shoes

est

Holiday fruitcakes

Chocolate-covered grasshoppers

IT SEEMED LIKE A GOOD IDEA AT THE TIME #4

"They are quite good, like avocado and new potato mixed."

> —University of Chicago professor Monte Lloyd, suggesting that residents of the city help stem one of the worst cicada infestations in years by cooking and eating the insects; he suggested deep frying the locustlike bugs in batter, or using them on pizzas, 1990

The Susan B. Anthony dollar

The swine flu vaccine

Savings and loan deregulation

The Watergate break-in

The Iran-contra affair

CIA domestic surveillance

Biological warfare

Vice President Dan Quayle

Vice President Spiro Agnew

IT SEEMED LIKE A GOOD IDEA AT THE TIME #5

"Follow me around. I don't care. I'm serious. If anybody wants to put a tail on me, go ahead."

> —Presidential candidate Gary Hart, defiantly suggesting to reporters that they try and verify rumors of his womanizing; reporters took him up on the idea and soon discovered he was apparently having an affair with model Donna Rice

IT SEEMED LIKE A GOOD IDEA AT THE TIME #6

"When you help the shepherd, you're helping the sheep. . . ."

> —Televangelist Jim Bakker, trying hard to
> seduce church secretary Jessica Hahn in a
> Florida motel room in 1980

IT SEEMED LIKE A GOOD IDEA AT THE TIME #7

"First I stopped a bicycle, cars, and a streetcar. Now I'm going to stop a train."

—Soviet psychic Yevgeny Frenkel, shortly
before he leaped in front of a speeding
freight train to prove he could halt it with
psychic energy; the train ran him over

Communism

Social Darwinism

Tax-and-spend liberalism

Trickle-down economics

Mob rule

Asbestos

Chlorofluorocarbons

Saccharin

The Dalkon Shield

Toxic-waste dumping

IT SEEMED LIKE A GOOD IDEA AT THE TIME #8

"DDT dusted in the hair is effective in controlling head lice. Pubic lice can also be readily brought under control with DDT powder. One ounce of DDT, dusted on the inside of the underwear, will kill all lice present. DDT can be used safely on your dog, too, to destroy fleas!"

> —Helpful household hints from the
> U.S. Department of Agriculture,
> 1947

IT SEEMED LIKE A GOOD IDEA AT THE TIME #9

"This is the best time in history for the pastime of atom-bomb watching. For the first time, the Atomic Energy Commission's Nevada test program will extend through the summer tourist season. And for the first time, the AEC has released a partial schedule, so that tourists interested in seeing a nuclear explosion can adjust their itineraries accordingly."

—Vacation ideas, from a 1957 *New York Times* travel article on the popularity and glamour of watching above-ground nuclear explosions ("You are there!") near Las Vegas

IT SEEMED LIKE A GOOD IDEA AT THE TIME #10

"I want to stop poverty, so people will cut trees and become rich."

> —A. Mendes, governor of Brazil's Amazon rain forest
> area, as he gave away five thousand power saws to
> settlers in the region so that they could cut down
> trees even faster; the gifts were seen as a concession
> to strong anti-environmental sentiment in the area,
> 1989

The DeLorean

The Spruce Goose

The "Star Wars" defense initiative

The arrangement of letters on typewriter keyboards

Prohibition

The Charge of the Light Brigade

The United States Football League

Welcoming the Trojan horse inside the city gates

Trying to fix the 1919 World Series

Lot's wife looking back to watch the destruction of Sodom

The attack on figure skater Nancy Kerrigan

Marathon dances

Polyester leisure suits

Goldfish swallowing

Smell-O-Vision movies

The Iraqi invasion of Kuwait

The U.S. selling arms to Iraq just before
the Iraqi invasion of Kuwait

IT SEEMED LIKE A GOOD IDEA AT THE TIME #11

"I must have a great victory! I must capture Moscow and amaze the world!"

> —Napoleon Bonaparte, in 1811; Napoleon's
> invasion of Russia eventually
> cost the lives of more than 400,000 of his
> troops (most of whom starved or froze to death)
> and led to his abdication as emperor of France

IT SEEMED LIKE A GOOD IDEA AT THE TIME #12

"Well, everybody has to get their hair cut. As you know, the president has a very busy schedule, and he just tries to work it in when he can."

> —White House spokesman George Stephanopoulos, trying to explain President Clinton's impulse to have his hair cut by Beverly Hills stylist Christophe, while Air Force One sat on the tarmac at Los Angeles International Airport, at a cost to taxpayers of thousands of dollars, 1993

The Salem witch trials

The Ku Klux Klan

Book burning

The musical version of *Lost Horizon*

The Crusades

The Inquisition

Geraldo Rivera

Eve eating the forbidden fruit

IT SEEMED LIKE A GOOD IDEA AT THE TIME #13

"We believe that present conditions are favorable for advantageous investment in standard American securities."

> —The giant U.S. investment firm
> Hornblower & Weeks, urging people to
> invest in the stock market, less than a week
> before the market took its biggest crash in
> history on October 29, 1929

IT SEEMED LIKE A GOOD IDEA AT THE TIME #14

"Anybody who has been to Strasburg can see that they can use some help."

> —Congressional spokeswoman Jean
> Broadshaug, defending the idea of using
> $500,000 in federal taxpayers' money to
> build a Lawrence Welk museum
> in Strasburg, North Dakota, 1990

IT SEEMED LIKE A GOOD IDEA AT THE TIME #15

"I'm sorry, Mr. Kipling, but you just don't know how to use the English language."

> —An editor at the *San Francisco Examiner*, trying to dissuade then 24-year-old Rudyard Kipling from pursuing a writing career, 1889

IT SEEMED LIKE A GOOD IDEA AT THE TIME #16

*"If something was offensive . . . we will not condone it, and
the people involved will be disciplined."*

> —USAir spokesman David Shipley, after two of the
> airline's flight attendants allegedly tried to "liven
> up" a dull flight from Pittsburgh to West Palm
> Beach by donning Arab headdresses and fake
> noses and pretending to be Middle East hijackers,
> 1991

IT SEEMED LIKE A GOOD IDEA AT THE TIME #17

"We have a new formula for Coke. It's a smoother, rounder, yet bolder taste."

—Coca-Cola chairman Roberto Goizueta, enthusiastically introducing the "new" Coke in 1985; despite the company's assertions that "This is the surest move ever made," they were forced by public demand to bring back the original Coke three months later

More Famous Bad Ideas

The Berlin Wall . . . *Ishtar* . . . The Bay of Pigs invasion . . .
Ollie North dolls . . . Phrenology . . . The king trying
to poison Hamlet . . . The House Committee on Un-
American Activities . . . The Battle of Actium . . . The
Reign of Terror . . . Caesar ignoring the Ides of March . . .
Bowdlerization . . . Whaling . . . The movie version of
Myra Breckinridge . . . Paroling Jack Henry Abbot . . .

Investing in Confederate war bonds . . .
Poll taxes . . . Human sacrifice . . . Towing icebergs
from Antarctica to Saudi Arabia to help satisfy
the Saudis' appetite for more fresh water . . .
The Vietnam War . . . The execution of Socrates . . .
Joan Crawford adopting children

To err is human . . .

—Alexander Pope